Guinea Pigs in Our Classroom

Josephine Masterson

Rosen REAL READERS

Rosen Classroom™
New York

We have guinea pigs
in our classroom.
Baby guinea pigs are called pups.

Our guinea pigs live in a cage.
We put hay in the cage.

Our guinea pigs like to sleep.

They sleep on hay.

We have male guinea pigs.
They are called boars.

We have female guinea pigs, too.
They are called sows.
Here is a mother with her pups.

Guinea pigs are vegetarians.
They do not eat meat.
We feed our guinea pigs plants.

We feed them vegetables, too.
Guinea pigs like to eat.

I hold our guinea pig.

I hold it carefully.

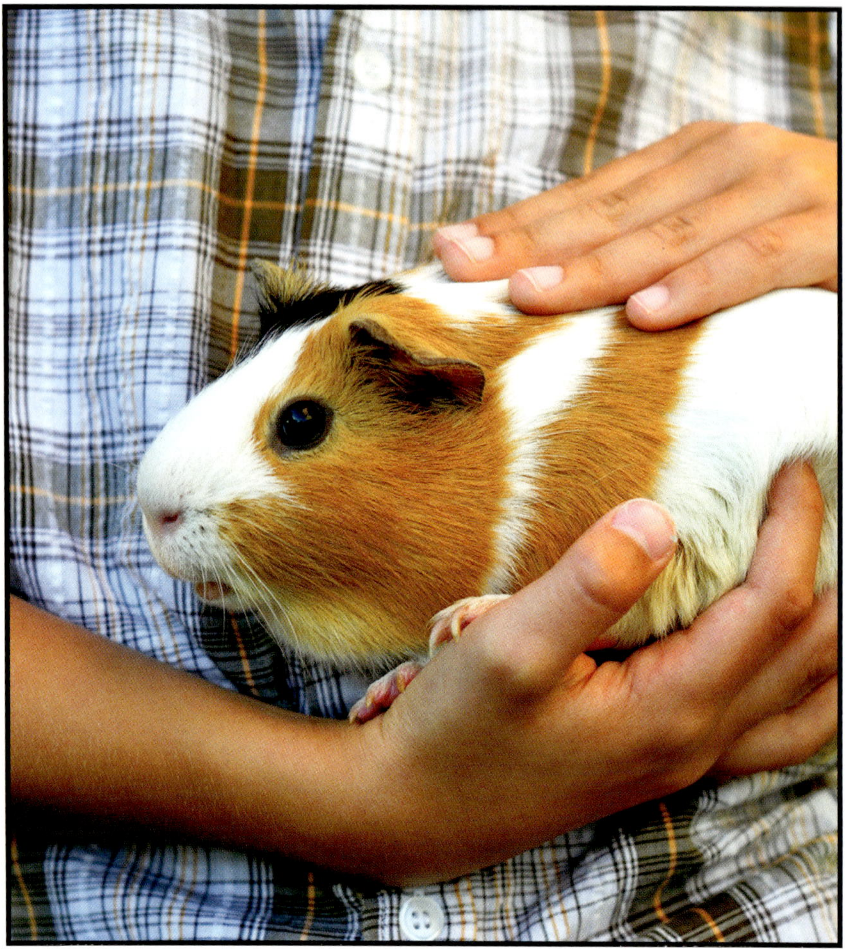

Guinea pigs like people.

We pet them.

They purr when they are happy.

We take our guinea pigs outside.

They play in the grass.

Words to Know

boar

cage

guinea pig

hay

pups

vegetables